Penguins

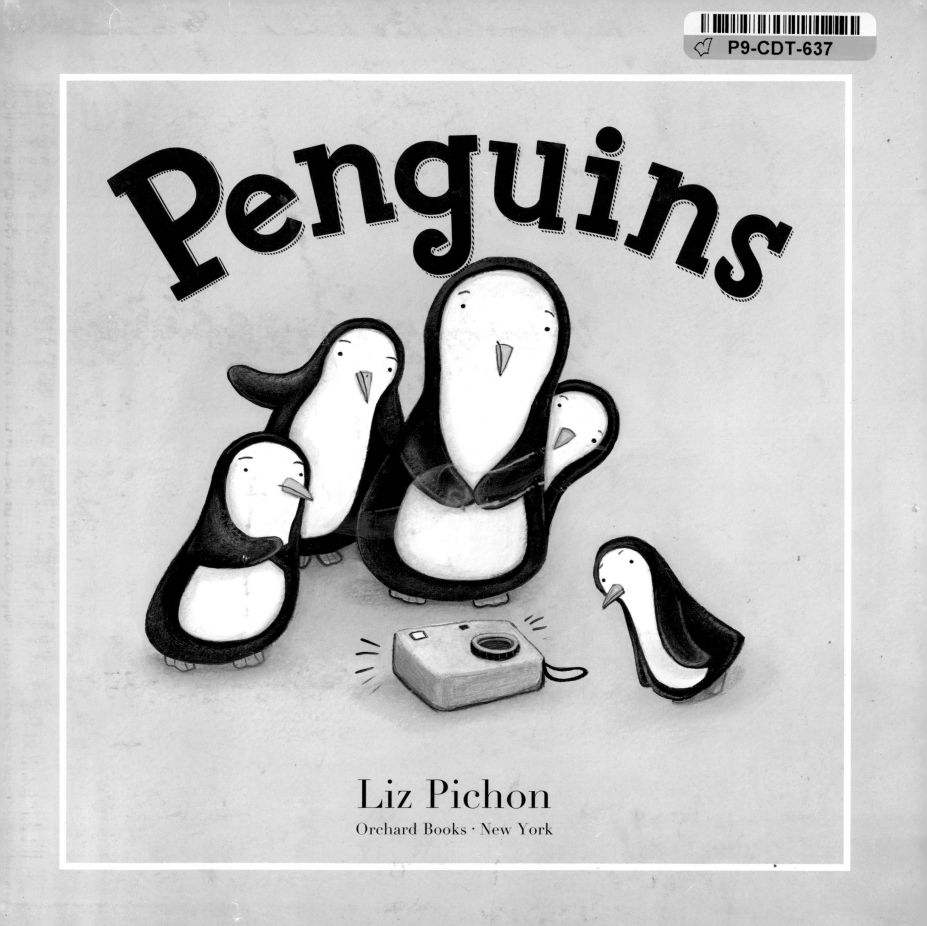

Liz Pichon

Orchard Books · New York

It's morning at the zoo.
The penguins wake up and have their first swim.

EVERYDAY PENGUIN ACTIVITIES

1. Swim.

2. Eat fish.

3. Play penguin games.

4. Sleep standing up.

5. Look at people.

6. Look at more people.

On rainy days, the penguins don't do much at all.

But when the sun shines and the people come, it's fun, fun, fun!

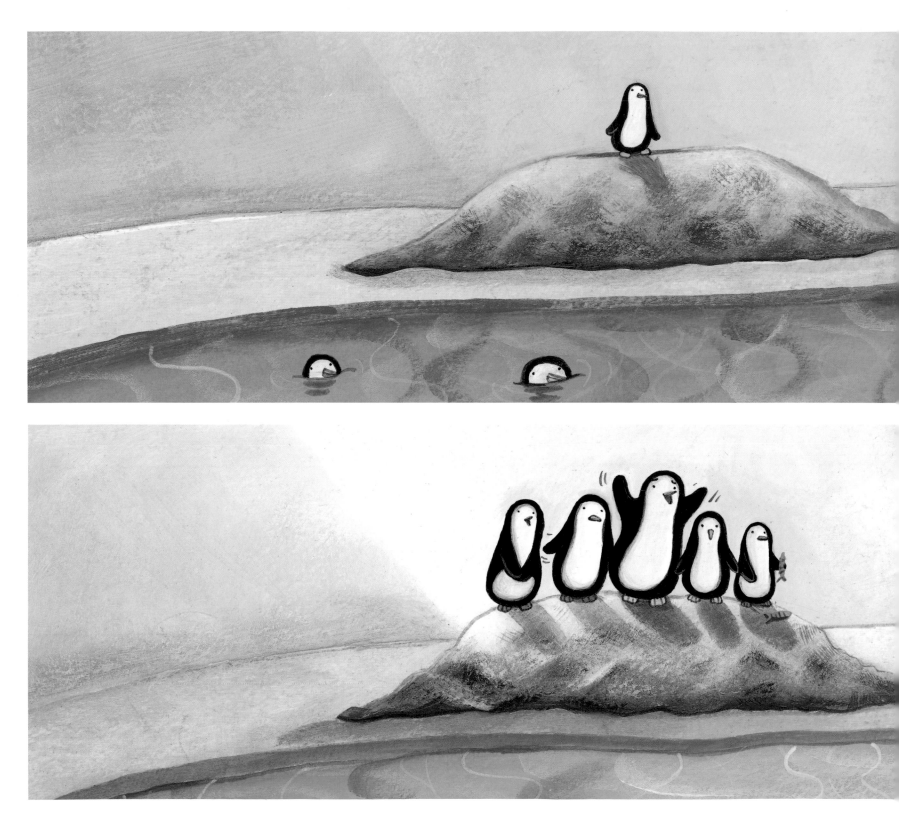

After all the people have gone, a little penguin notices something. "DON'T TOUCH IT!" says his mother. "Somebody will be back for it."

But nobody comes back.
The little penguin moves closer for a better look.

He goes over and picks it up.
"It's a camera!" says the little penguin.
"What do you do with a camera?" the other penguins ask.
"You smile at it!" says the little penguin, grinning.

"Are you sure you can't eat it?" asks a hungry penguin.

A baby penguin jumps on the camera and says, "Let's press ALL the buttons!"

FLASH!

They all get bug eyes.

"Everyone waddle over there and line up," says the little penguin.

"Okay," they reply.

The little penguin looks through
the camera lens.

"What do we do?"
shout all the other penguins.

The little penguin puts his flipper
on the button and says,
"Everyone look at me and say FISH!"

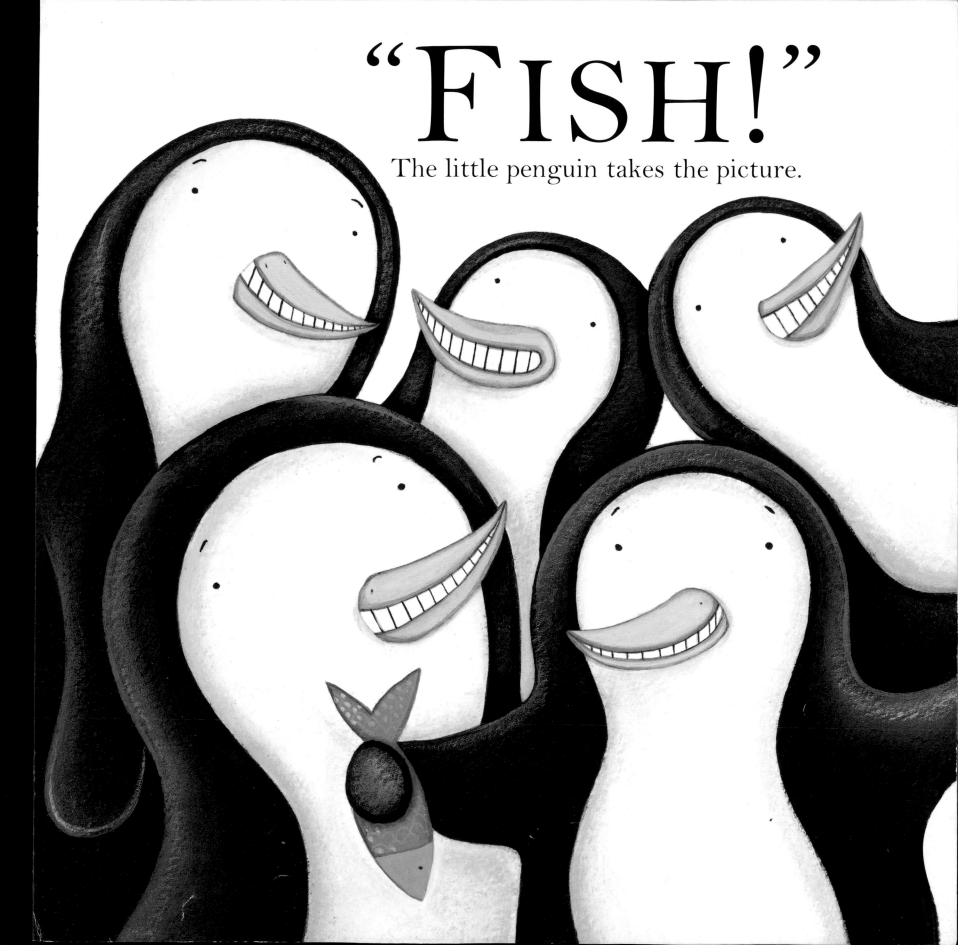

"FISH!"

The little penguin takes the picture.

Now all the penguins
want to use the camera.

They take lots and lots
of amazing pictures.

But suddenly…

… the camera stops working!

"Oh, dear," says the mother penguin, "you'd better put it back now."

So the little penguin puts the camera back on the rock where he found it.

The next morning the zookeeper sees the camera. "What's this doing here?" he says. "I'd better take it to lost and found."

Soon the camera is returned to the little girl who dropped it.

"Your camera is not broken," says the zookeeper,
"but the penguins seem to have pecked it a bit."

"That's okay!" the little girl replies. "I love penguins!"

A few days later the pictures are developed.
There are pictures of monkeys, lions, tigers,
and elephants. And, strangely, there are
quite a few pictures of penguins, too!